Before reading

Look at the b…
Ask, "What d…

Turn to the **Key…** …d with
the child. Draw … noting
the tall letters a…

During read…

Offer plenty of support and praise as the child reads the story. Listen carefully and respond to events in the text.

When a **Key Word** is used for the first time, it is also shown at the bottom of the page. If the child hesitates over a word, point to the **New Key Words** box and practise reading it together. If the word is phonically decodable, you can sound out the letters and blend the sounds to read the word ("d-o-g, dog"). Praise the child for their effort, then return to the story.

Pause every few pages and ask questions to check the child's understanding of what they have read. If they begin to lose concentration, stop reading and save the page for later.

Celebrate the child's achievement and come back to the story the next day.

After reading

After reading this book, ask, "Did you enjoy the story? What did you like about it?" Encourage the child to share their opinions.

Use the comprehension questions on page 54 to check the child's understanding and recall of the text.

Ladybird

Series Consultant: Professor David Waugh
With thanks to Kulwinder Maude

LADYBIRD BOOKS

UK | USA | Canada | Ireland | Australia
India | New Zealand | South Africa

Ladybird Books is part of the Penguin Random House group of companies whose addresses can be found at global.penguinrandomhouse.com.
www.penguin.co.uk www.puffin.co.uk www.ladybird.co.uk

Penguin Random House UK

Original edition of Key Words with Peter and Jane first published by Ladybird Books Ltd 1964
Series updated 2023
This book first published 2023
001

Illustrations by Martyn Cain
Based on characters and design by Gustavo Mazali

With thanks to Liz Pemberton for her contributions in advising on the illustrations
With thanks to Inclusive Minds for connecting us with their Inclusion Ambassador network, and in particular thanks to Guntaas Kaur Chugh for her input on the illustrations

Printed in China

The authorized representative in the EEA is Penguin Random House Ireland, Morrison Chambers, 32 Nassau Street, Dublin D02 YH68

A CIP catalogue record for this book is available from the British Library

ISBN: 978-0-241-51097-1

All correspondence to:
Ladybird Books
Penguin Random House Children's
One Embassy Gardens, 8 Viaduct Gardens, London SW11 7BW

FSC
www.fsc.org
MIX
Paper from responsible sources
FSC® C018179

Key Words

with Peter and Jane

9a

Aunt Liz and Uncle Jack

Based on the original
Key Words with Peter and Jane
reading scheme and research by William Murray

Original edition written by William Murray
This edition written by James Clements
Illustrated by Martyn Cain
Based on characters and design by Gustavo Mazali

Key Words

always another back buy

call could did dinner fast

found head homework just

kite learn may money

Mr Mrs never new over

place road should teacher

think too way well were

why wish would write

dinner

head

homework

kite

money

road

teacher

write

Peter and Jane were on their way to Aunt Liz and Uncle Jack's house. They were pleased to be going there.

They were all going to have dinner. After that, Mum, Dad and Tess were going home. Jane and Peter were going to stay for another few days.

Dad wanted to find a new way of getting there.

New Key Words

were way dinner
another new

"Why don't we go the way we always go? Do you know this way?" asked Mum.

Jane and Peter did not think that Dad *did* know this way.

"I think it's that way," said Dad, turning the car into another road.

Mum shook her head.

New Key Words

why always did think road head

"Aunt Liz and Uncle Jack's place should be just this way. It should be just up here," said Dad, as he turned into a new road next to the beach.

"I can see kites on the beach!" said Peter.

Dad turned the car into another road. It was Aunt Liz and Uncle Jack's road! Dad had found their place.

"Well, you found it!" said Mum.

"I did," said Dad.

New Key Words

place should just kite found well

Peter and Jane hugged Aunt Liz and Uncle Jack, and Tess sniffed their dog, Kit.

"It is always so good to see you," said Aunt Liz. "You all look so well!"

"You got here fast!" said Uncle Jack.

"I found a new way to get here," said Dad, as he headed back to the car to get the bags.

New Key Words

fast back

“Would you like to have dinner now?” asked Aunt Liz.

“Yes, we would like dinner now, please!” Peter and Jane said.

They were pleased that it was time for dinner. Aunt Liz worked in a cafe, so she always cooked good dishes.

“Uncle Jack always says that I have too many cookbooks,” said Aunt Liz, “but there are always new dishes to learn!”

New Key Words

would too learn

At dinner, Aunt Liz chatted to the children about some of the things they could do on holiday.

"Could we go and see the kites on the beach one day?" asked Peter.

"Yes, we can!" said Aunt Liz.

"We should go to the new cafe for dinner too," said Uncle Jack.

"I think this holiday should be really fun," Peter said to Jane.

New Key Words

could

After dinner, Mum and Dad said they would go back home. They gave Peter and Jane a little money to buy some things on their holiday.

"Thank you for the money!" said Peter. "I think I'm going to buy a new stunt kite. Stunt kites can go very fast and do tricks."

Jane could not think what to buy with her money. She never could!

New Key Words

money buy never

Mum said the children should learn their spellings really well, and they should do their holiday homework.

"You should write down all the things you do here in your homework books," said Mum. "Your teachers would like to read what you did on holiday."

Mum, Dad and Tess crossed over the road to the car.

"Please call us every day," said Dad.

"We will!" Peter and Jane called back.

New Key Words

homework write
teacher over call

Soon, it was time for bed. Before going to sleep, Peter and Jane chatted to Aunt Liz about their teachers, Mr Bell and Mrs Rahim.

"Mr Bell is my teacher," said Jane.

"My teacher is Mrs Rahim," said Peter.

"I think your teachers will be pleased if you do your homework well," said Aunt Liz.

"We will do it well," they said.

New Key Words

Mr Mrs

The next day, Peter asked Uncle Jack if he could go to the shops to buy a stunt kite.

"Why don't you take Kit over to the woods for a walk first?" asked Aunt Liz.

"You should get your trainers," said Uncle Jack.

"Why?" asked Peter.

"You'll see why," said Uncle Jack.

New Key Words

At the woods, Kit zoomed all over the place. He jumped over logs and roots. Peter and Jane had to run very fast just to keep up. Peter was glad that he had his trainers on!

"Kit just never slows down. I wish I could run just as fast as him!" said Peter.

"What would happen if Kit was too fast and you could not find him?" Jane asked Uncle Jack.

Uncle Jack said that Kit always did come back.

New Key Words

wish

Back at home, Aunt Liz asked, "What did you learn in the woods?"

"We learned that Kit is very fast!" said Peter. "I am going to write about him in my homework for Mrs Rahim."

After Peter and Jane did their homework, Aunt Liz said, "Why don't we go to the city and buy your kite now, Peter? Bring your money. You too, Jane."

New Key Words

Aunt Liz found a place to buy Peter's kite. It was called Mr Smith's Toy Shop.

"Do you have a stunt kite?" Peter asked Mr Smith.

Mr Smith did not have a stunt kite, but he showed Peter another kite.

"Why not get this bird kite?" asked Mr Smith. "It is very fast."

Peter did not want to buy that kite.

New Key Words

Peter and Jane walked all over the city, looking in one shop after another. Peter started to think he would never find a stunt kite.

"I wish just one place had a stunt kite," he said.

"I think I may know one more place, but it's on another road," said Aunt Liz. "Let's get a cold drink in this place first."

New Key Words

may

Gold

After buying drinks, they walked over the road and down another street. There, they found another shop called Mrs May's Models.

Mrs May looked at the back of her shop and found a stunt kite.

"This kite is not new," Mrs May said, "but it should still work well."

"It's just what I want!" Peter said. He gave Mrs May his money.

"Good. I think it's time for us to head back home," said Aunt Liz.

New Key Words

On the way back, they walked past a bookshop. There was a cookbook to buy in the window.

"Wow!" said Aunt Liz. "I have always wanted that book. I have been looking for it all over the place."

"Why don't you buy it?" asked Jane.

"I'll come back and buy it another time," said Aunt Liz. "It's good to know that it's here."

New Key Words

KSHOP

After dinner, Aunt Liz did the washing up. Peter and Jane were learning some new spellings from Mr Bell and Mrs Rahim.

"How did I do?" asked Peter.

"You did well!" said Jane. "But there are still many more spellings for you to learn."

After that, Peter called Mum and Dad to tell them that he had found a new kite at Mrs May's shop.

New Key Words

The next day, Aunt Liz was at work. Uncle Jack said they should go and call on Tom and Erin.

Erin and her dad, Tom, lived next door to Aunt Liz and Uncle Jack. Erin and Tom liked the sea, and they were always out in their boat.

"Why don't we all head out on the boat today?" asked Tom. "Would you like that?"

"Yes, please!" said Peter and Jane.

New Key Words

On the boat, Peter wished that they could go faster.

"We never go fast near the beach," Tom said.

"Why not?" asked Peter.

"Because there could be swimmers there," said Tom.

But out at sea, Tom gave Peter his wish. "Now we can go faster, Peter!" Tom said.

New Key Words

Tom said that they should head back now.

“That was good fun! I just wish we could come back again,” said Peter.

“We may come back another day,” said Tom.

“Please can we, Tom?” asked Peter and Jane. “We would like that.”

New Key Words

Back at the flat, Aunt Liz was cooking dinner. Peter was going to learn his spellings for Mrs Rahim, but Jane and Uncle Jack were putting on their coats.

"Why are you putting on your coats?" Aunt Liz asked them. "Jane should do her homework for her teacher before dinner."

"Jane and I are just heading out for a bit," said Uncle Jack. "We will be back soon."

New Key Words

Aunt Liz sat down with Peter.

"Mrs Rahim's spellings are hard!" Peter said.

"I'll help you learn them," said Aunt Liz. "You may want to write them in your homework book."

Very soon, Jane and Uncle Jack walked back into the flat.

"Did you have a good walk?" asked Aunt Liz.

"Yes, we just walked down the road to the bookshop," said Uncle Jack.

New Key Words

Jane had found something to buy with her money.

"We walked back to the shop so that I could buy you the cookbook you were looking at," said Jane.

"Wow, thank you, Jane! You are really kind," said Aunt Liz. "I will make you something from my new cookbook."

"I'm very pleased that we're staying for another few days!" said Peter.

New Key Words

Questions

Answer these questions about the story.

1 What does Dad want to do on the way to Aunt Liz and Uncle Jack's house?

2 Where does Aunt Liz work?

3 What does Peter want to buy at the shops?

4 Why do you think Uncle Jack tells Peter to put on his trainers?

5 What do Jane, Peter and Uncle Jack do with Tom and Erin?

6 What does Jane buy with her money at the end of the story?